The Adventures of
Benny and Watch™

WATCH RUNS AWAY

Created by **Gertrude Chandler Warner**

Illustrated by **Daniel Mark Duffy**

ALBERT WHITMAN & Company
Morton Grove, Illinois

You will also want to read:
Meet the Boxcar Children
A Present for Grandfather
Benny's New Friend
The Magic Show Mystery
Benny Goes Into Business

Library of Congress Cataloging-in-Publication Data

Warner, Gertrude Chandler, 1890–1979
Watch runs away / created by Gertrude Chandler Warner;
illustrated by Daniel Mark Duffy.
p.   cm. — (The adventures of Benny and Watch)
Summary: Benny tries to figure out why his dog,
Watch, keeps escaping from the yard
ISBN 0-8075-8681-1 (paperback)
[1. Dogs—Fiction.] I. Duffy, Daniel M., ill. II. Title.
PZ7.W244Wat   1999
[E]—dc21   98-54892
CIP
AC

Copyright © 1999 by Albert Whitman & Company.
Published in 1999 by Albert Whitman & Company,
6340 Oakton Street, Morton Grove, Illinois 60053.
Published simultaneously in Canada by
General Publishing, Limited, Toronto.

The Boxcar Children

Henry, Jessie, Violet, and Benny Alden are orphans. They are supposed to live with their grandfather, but they have heard that he is mean. So the children run away and live in an old red boxcar. They find a dog, and Benny names him Watch.

When Grandfather finds them, the children see that he is not mean at all. They happily go to live with him. And, as a surprise, Grandfather brings the boxcar along!

Everyone in the Alden family
loved Watch. But Watch was Benny's
best friend. They did everything
together.

Every morning, Benny put food and water in Watch's bowls. He whistled for Watch. They played all day.

One morning, Benny whistled, but his dog didn't leap up the steps. "Here, Watch!" Benny called.

Benny waited.

A few minutes later, Watch raced up on the porch.

"Where have you been?" Benny asked.

Watch just licked Benny's face.

"Your paws have yellow mud on them," Benny said. The dirt in Mrs. McGregor's flower beds was brown. Somehow Watch had gotten out of the yard.

Benny looked at the fence. It went
all around the yard. The gate was locked.
How did his dog get out?

Maybe Watch climbed the fence. Benny put his feet between the boards and climbed over the top.

But Watch just stood there and whined. He couldn't climb that high.

What was going on? Could a dog have a secret? Tomorrow Benny would follow Watch.

The next morning, Benny opened the door. Watch bounded down the steps. Benny ran down the steps, too.

Watch raced to a bush by the fence. He crawled under the bush and . . . disappeared!

What was going on? Could a dog have a secret? Tomorrow Benny would follow Watch.

The next morning, Benny opened the door. Watch bounded down the steps. Benny ran down the steps, too.

Watch raced to a bush by the fence. He crawled under the bush and . . . disappeared!

Benny looked under the bush.
Watch had dug a hole under the
fence. The dog could wiggle through,
but Benny was too big. By the time
Benny went through the gate, his dog
was long gone.

"Watch keeps running away," Benny told Henry.

"How does he get out?" asked Violet.

"He dug a hole under the fence," Benny said.

"Where does Watch go?" Jessie asked.

"I don't know," said Benny.

There was only one way to find out. He would follow Watch again. *This* time he would stay on his dog's trail.

The next day, Watch ran outside
and wiggled under the fence. Benny
hurried through the gate. Watch was in
their neighbor's yard. Benny raced to
catch him.

Watch trotted across lawns.
Benny trotted across lawns.

Watch ducked
down an alley.
Benny ducked
down an alley.

It was hard to keep up. Watch was a lot faster than Benny.

Watch squeezed under a loose fence board.

Benny squeezed under a loose fence board.

It took a long time.

On the other side was
a grassy field. Watch ran
like the wind.

Watch was so far
ahead that Benny couldn't
see where he had gone.
So Benny went home.

After breakfast, Violet said to Benny, "You didn't eat much. What's wrong?"

"I went after Watch," Benny said. "He ran away again. He doesn't like me anymore."

"But Watch is your best friend," said Jessie.

Benny's face was sad. "Maybe Watch has a new best friend," he said.

Watch came home later.

Henry filled in the hole. "Don't worry," he told Benny. "Watch won't leave again."

But Henry was wrong. The next morning, there was a new hole. Watch had run away again.

Benny wondered if his dog would come back this time. Maybe Watch didn't want to live with them anymore. Maybe he'd found a new family.

Then Benny had an idea. Every time Watch came home, his feet were dirty with yellow mud. The yellow mud would lead Benny to Watch's secret place!

Clumps were by the fence. Benny found more clumps in their neighbor's yard.

There wasn't much mud in the alley or by the loose fence board.

But Watch had worn a path in the grassy field.

Benny ran down the path. He came
upon an old shed. The door hung open.
"Hello," Benny called.

"RUFF!"

Inside, a dog barked.
Watch!

Benny pushed the door open. He saw his dog in a corner, lying on a pile of rags. All around Watch were kittens! Gray kittens, black kittens, and striped kittens played around Benny's dog.

"Watch!" Benny cried. "What are you doing?"

Just then a cat walked in. Watch got up carefully so he wouldn't hurt the kittens. The mother cat lay down and began washing her babies. Benny and Watch left the shed.

When they got home, Benny ran to his brother and sisters. "Guess where I found Watch!" he exclaimed. "Baby-sitting kittens!"

"Kittens? Aren't cats and dogs enemies?" Violet asked.

"Animals don't always act the way we think they should," Henry said.

"That mother cat probably doesn't have a home," Jessie said.

"We'll find her a home," said Violet.

"And all the kittens," added Benny.

Benny gave Watch a hug.

He was glad Watch didn't have a new family. But it was okay for his dog to have *two* families, just for a little while!